Eternal Kiss

A New Orleans Vampire King Novella

By Faith Gibson

CHAPTER ONE

Lukas

THE HIGHBALL GLASS shattered in my hand. I stared at the shards mixed with blood and bourbon. Blood was my life's essence, and mine was dripping onto the Persian rug under my desk chair. I, Lukas Benoit, was one of the deadliest beings in the southeast, but somehow, I had failed my progeny. Douglas Caan was not only my made child but also my best friend. Hell, he was my only friend, but that was by my own design. Trust didn't come easy to my kind, and he was one of few I offered mine. The fact that he and I had been more than boss and employee was a secret no one should have known unless he had slipped. There was no reason for his death other than to hurt me. I was still reeling from his murder and would be for a long time.

Where Lucifer had his demons who mostly remained in the underworld, Lillith created a different type of being. Ones who could roam the earth without being summoned. As an Ancient, I could create my own kind, though I chose not to do so often. There were plenty of vampires who had been made, and corralling the bastards was a full-time job. Jealousy as well as greed for power, money, and territory was rampant. I had it all in spades, everything except jealousy. To the made vamps in my territory, I was the boss and had been since I took the southeast from a weak bastard named Constantine more than three hundred years ago.

I did not take kindly to failure, and when it was my own? Unacceptable. I failed Doug, and that was the wakeup call I needed. I had become lax, but no more.

Two brisk knocks rapped on my door before my assistant entered my office. "Hey, Boss. A Daniel Field— What happened?" Arabella rushed to my side, but I waved her off.

I stood and moved to the bathroom, dropping the glass fragments not embedded in my palm into the waste basket, then shoved my hand under the cold water. "Finish what you were going to tell me."

"Daniel Fielding, an attorney, left a message for you regarding The Limelight."

I glanced over my shoulder, narrowing my eyes. Anyone else would shrink at my anger, but Arabella had been with me for almost forty years. She was used to my snarls and sharp tongue. "What about it?" On paper, Doug had purchased the club from me, but in truth, I had gifted The Limelight, New Orleans' premier jazz club, to him. Even though he had owned the joint, he spent most nights playing saxophone until the early morning hours, garnering a huge following.

"Mr. Fielding contacted Mr. Caan's next of kin, requesting her presence for the reading of the will."

I turned off the water and began extracting glass from my palm before the skin had a chance to heal around it. Doug's next of kin was a daughter he'd left behind when I turned him. He disappeared from her life, so it would be interesting to see how she handled the news that she now owned The Limelight as well as his house in the Garden District and a shit-ton of money. Not the billions I had acquired but enough that she was set for life.

"Did he say when he expects her?" I rinsed my hand again. While drying it, I turned to Arabella, waiting for an answer.

"She's already in town. Their appointment is tomorrow morning. He was calling to see if you could meet her at the club this afternoon. He left her contact information in the message."

"Very well. Call Dinah and ask her to meet me there at two."

3

It was Arabella's turn to frown. "You know her name?"

Fuck. I needed to get my shit together. It wasn't like me to slip up, even in front of my assistant. Especially in front of her. I had made the mistake of fucking her many years ago, and even though I made it clear it was a one-time deal, she often hinted at us being something more. Maybe it was time to get a new assistant.

"Of course I know her name," I hissed. "I learn everything about a person before I turn them, or have you forgotten?"

Arabella inclined her head. "My apologies, Boss. I'll call Miss Caan now." Stopping at the door, she pointed to the rug. "Would you like me to take care of that?"

"No. I'll handle it. I have calls to make, so do not disturb me again." I wouldn't allow anyone to have access to my blood, even if it was a few drops, especially in a city where magic was practiced on the regular. Once Arabella closed the door behind her, I moved my chair and pulled the rug away from my desk, rolling it up. One benefit of being wealthy was owning numerous businesses around the city, one of which was a funeral parlor equipped with a crematory in the basement. It came in handy for burning rugs containing my blood or people who needed to disappear. Although I used a secret exit only I knew about, I glamoured myself. None of my coven knew I was an Ancient nor that I could compel them as well as I could a human. It was why Arabella didn't question how I was able to meet Dinah during the day.

Since I had a couple of hours before meeting with Dinah, I made the funeral parlor my first stop. I used my key and entered the basement where I burned the rug myself. Once that task was completed, I drove to the Quarter and parked at one of the many houses I owned. Then I strolled the busy sidewalks, stopping for a cup of chicory coffee. Unlike a made vamp, I could eat and drink human food. I could walk in the daylight. I couldn't be killed by a stake, wooden or otherwise. A bullet to the heart did nothing more than piss me off because it ruined the bespoke suit I wore like armor. There was only one way to permanently end an Ancient, and that was to take my head. The only ones alive, or undead, who knew this were other Ancients unless said Ancients had shared, which would be beyond foolish. We didn't live forever if we couldn't keep our mouths shut, and I knew my brothers well. They were as tight-lipped as I was.

I could create vampires, but I couldn't bestow them with my gifts. It's why Doug was dead. Permanently. Per his wishes, I had gathered his ashes that now resided in a gilded urn engraved with a saxophone. He had been killed with a wooden stake made from a baobab tree, which was ironic considering it was referred to as the tree of life. That was another reason I was pissed. Where the fuck would a local vamp get the sacred wood? My mind had been in turmoil ever since I found Doug's ashes amid the clothes he'd worn that night. It was one reason I walked the streets of my city glamoured. I visited every haunt of my coven. I eavesdropped on whispered conversations. I followed at night as they hunted their next meal. Eight days later, and I was no closer to finding the killer.

As I neared the club, I moved out of the way of pedestrians. Humans could be rude if you stopped for no apparently good reason. Little did they know I could end them with a word. Some days, I was tempted. I wanted to get a look at Doug's daughter before introducing myself. Another of his wishes was that if anything happened to him, all his assets went to her. Lillith knew I didn't need the club or his house or his money, but handing it all over to the child he hadn't seen in almost thirty years was going to be a pain in my ass. Back when I gifted The Limelight to Doug, I needed something to fill my time, so I acted as manager, changing my name and appearance every decade or so. Another of Doug's wishes was for me to remain manager if Dinah decided to keep the club instead of selling it. I would do anything for him, so I agreed.

I approached wearing the glamour of Luke Bennett, manager. Yes, it was close to me true name, but reinventing myself was also a pain in the ass. My tailor-made suit appeared as one off-the-rack. My perfectly styled hair was now messy, and my sharp facial features were somewhat rounded and mundane. A woman stood at the door, reading the sign that stated we were closed until further notice, and I devoured her from head to toe.

There was no way *this* was Doug's daughter. Lillith wouldn't be so cruel.

"Dinah?"

She turned at her name. The creature in front of me was a fucking goddess. Long dark hair. Curves for days. Full lips. Bedroom eyes. In other words, my kryptonite. If I could dress her in a Victorian gown, I would bury my face between her full breasts and… *Damn you, Lillith.* I'd known about Dinah Caan, the young daughter Doug left behind in Tennessee, but I hadn't been aware of how alluring she would be all grown up. Let's just say this was not going to end well for one of us.

"I'm Luke Bennett," I introduced myself and held out my hand. Dinah placed her palm against mine. Instead of a quick shake, she held on as her eyes roamed down my body. I was used to the attention, even glamoured, but coming from her it was akin to being kissed by the sun on a cold day. Her skin flushed when she noticed my smirk.

Dinah removed her hand from mine, which was a pity. "It's a pleasure to meet you, Luke."

"My deepest condolences. Doug was a good man." I shoved my hands in my pants pockets to keep from grabbing her and sinking my fangs into her neck.

Her countenance changed from flirty to serious. "Doug was a stranger to me. He left when I was six, and I haven't seen him since. You obviously knew a different Doug Caan than I did."

I wanted to explain the man Doug had been. The one she didn't know, but now wasn't the time. When I failed to say anything, she continued, "I apologize for being insensitive to your feelings. I'm sorry for your loss."

"Thank you. Let's step inside and get out of the foot traffic." I pulled the keys from my pocket, unlocked the door, and ushered Dinah inside. Her steps were hesitant as she looked around.

"I called in a cleaning crew as soon as the club was released by the detective. I didn't want you to see the place in disarray," I told her. I had called in a crew after I gathered Doug's ashes, and then I'd had to get creative, finding a body to show the detective while compelling

8

him that the homeless person was Doug Caan. If it hadn't been for Dinah inheriting the club, I wouldn't have bothered. "In all honestly, I could have opened the club a couple nights ago, but I didn't want to step on any toes." I moved behind the bar and poured myself a drink. "Can I get you anything?"

"I'll have water, please." Dinah sat across from me on one of the stools and wrapped her hands around the glass when I placed it on the bar. "I have no knowledge of running an establishment such as this. I earned a degree in business, but I currently work in marketing for a major music producer."

"Please don't worry about the day-to-day operations. I've been overseeing The Limelight for almost a decade, and unless you have someone in mind to take my place, I would love to continue in that capacity." I dropped my voice and said, "You should sell the bar to me."

Dinah shivered at the compulsion, but she quickly shook it off. "I would like to take some time and think about that."

Interesting. "I have put together several documents, which outline my roll and compensation within the organization as well as all the other employees. I've also included a document listing weekly costs versus revenue." I produced a ledger from behind the bar and placed it in front of her. Call me old school, but I still used pen and paper before transferring the numbers to a computer program.

"Please feel free to reopen as soon as possible. I'll want to take a more thorough look at what you've prepared, but I don't see the need to change anything with regards to how the club is managed. I appreciate the ledger, but I'd like an electronic version as well."

"I will open the club as soon as I contact all our employees, and if you give me your email address, I'll send you all the information you need to make a decision." She gave me her email which I typed into my phone. Then I did the most asinine thing I'd managed in several centuries. "Now that business is out of the way, what do you say to dinner? I would love to show you around our city. Well, at least the French Quarter. We won't have time to see everything New Orleans has to offer, but..." I clamped my mouth shut. What the fuck was I doing? I needed to get away from the vixen, not spend more time with her, but as I mentioned earlier, her type was my kryptonite. I had bedded hundreds of females and even a few males over the millennia I'd been on Earth, but none had struck me the way Dinah Caan did. I wanted her like I'd never wanted anything.

"I would love to go to dinner with you. I can meet you back here around six, if that's okay."

I didn't want Dinah wandering the Quarter alone. "Six is perfect, but I'd like to pick you up at your hotel if you don't mind?"

She flashed a brilliant smile my way. "I don't mind. I'm staying at Caesar's. Text me when you get there, and I'll meet you in the lobby."

"It's a date." Seriously? Who the fuck had taken over my body? I was acting like a schoolboy instead of the badass I was. Maybe Dinah was a witch and had cast a spell on me. There was no other reason for me to behave so far outside the norm. Dinah stuffed the ledger into her messenger bag and slid from the stool. She walked away without looking back.

I pulled on a different glamour, locked the club, and followed her. For all she knew, I was her employee, nothing more. She had no prior knowledge of her father's club or other assets. She had no idea how a talented saxophone player became the owner of the biggest hotspot on Bourbon Street. How he amassed such wealth in his fifty-five years. If I had my way, she would never know. Some truths were better left buried with the dead.

Dinah strolled along the busy sidewalks, glancing at displays in windows. I followed at a distance, stopping when she did. To the people around me, I was another tourist. Even the residents and business owners of New

11

Orleans saw me as some mundane human with ill-fitting clothes, shaggy hair, and thick glasses. As an Ancient, I could become anyone at any time. I had been tempted to show my true visage to Dinah, but better sense kept me from doing so. No one other than my brothers knew the real me, not even those of my kind including Arabella, so why did I want Dinah to see me in all my vampire glory?

Was I replacing one Caan with another? Did I think Dinah could fill the void left by her father? Maybe somewhere deep in my subconscious I did. It had to be the reason I asked her to dinner. I needed to stay away from the raven-haired beauty. I needed to convince her I could run the club without her interference, sending her back to Nashville. Then again, just the thought of her leaving my city had my fangs itching to drop. To remake her. To claim her as my own. Never in my thousands of years had I wanted a queen. Unlike most of my brothers, I ruled alone. Always had. Dinah froze, her heart beating erratically. Every pulse resonated within me, causing my fangs to ache and my sharp nails threatening to lengthen. I pulled back my power, and she took off. Instead of following her to the hotel, I called the front desk and asked for her room number. Under normal circumstances, they shouldn't have divulged a guest's information, but when I asked for something, I got it. Once I had the information, I detoured to a local floral shop, ordering two dozen red roses, where I personally wrote a brief message on the card, then once again used compulsion to convince the clerk to have them delivered immediately.

I stood outside the hotel, sipping a café au lait, staring at the higher floors. I had no idea what side of the building Dinah was on until I caught sight of her in one of the windows. Her presence called to me like a siren, and that was the push I needed to walk away. I used my free time to stroll along the Quarter. Being late October, the residents had decorated for Halloween, each representation more elaborate than the next. Not as prevalent as Mardi Gras, the holiday still brought in plenty of tourists to boost the economy. Two young boys busked at a corner, and I slowed long enough to drop some bills in their tip basket. The youngest one thanked me with a gap-toothed grin, never slowing his drumming hands. I winked at him and continued on my way.

Instead of going home, I retrieved my car and drove to Doug's house. It wouldn't be long before Dinah took possession of the property, and it would break my cold, dead heart if she sold it. It too had been my gift to my progeny. I stepped inside, and what I found nearly broke me.

CHAPTER TWO

Dinah

I STOPPED IN front of the locked door of The Limelight, and a chill formed goosebumps on my arms, even in the southern heat. It had been over a week since a murder was committed after hours inside the jazz club. I had expected to see crime scene tape covering the entrance, but there was none. Candles lined the sidewalk along with other items paying their respects to the victim. There was a note on the door stating the club was closed until further notice. I was still in shock to learn that Kirkland Douglas Caan, owner and saxophonist of one of the most sought-after pieces of real estate in New Orleans, had been gunned down by an unknown suspect. If I were one of the residents of the city, one of many who enjoyed jazz music inside the club, I might also have lit a candle. But I wasn't one of those people. I was Doug Caan's only child.

As such, I now owned what most would consider a

legacy passed down from one generation to the next. The father I barely remembered left the place, along with all his assets, to me. The detective said Doug was in the wrong place at the wrong time, but was he really? Since he owned the jazz club and spent every night there, he could have been right where he was supposed to be when the bullet found his chest.

My mother often waxed poetic about the man who swept her off her feet, but I never understood how she could forgive him for abandoning us. Abandoning me. He had been my hero. The dad who tucked me in before leaving at night to play in whatever club hired him. Then he up and left before I turned seven without so much as a goodbye. I spent months waiting for him to return. Months crying when it was time to go to bed without his kiss to the forehead. He had sent cards at Christmas and my birthday filled with a sizeable check. Did he think they made up for his absence? They didn't, and neither did this dark building with its secrets. There had been a riot outside the club where he was playing the night he disappeared. My mother assured me when I was older that had nothing to do with Dad leaving town, but what if he wasn't who she thought he was?

"Dinah?"

I turned at my name and found myself face-to-face with the most striking man I'd ever seen in my twenty-eight years. "Yes?" I managed to breathe out.

"I'm Luke Bennett," the man drawled in a sensuous accent. All previous interactions had been through my father's attorney, save for the phone call earlier setting this appointment. I had expected the manager of Doug's club – my club – to be my father's age. This man was early thirties at most. He held out his hand for me to shake. I placed mine in his and was shocked at the coolness of his skin. Still, I never wanted to let go.

Working in the music industry in Nashville put me in the presence of beautiful men and women, but Luke was in a class all his own. And he had class in spades. He wore a dark grey suit that fit him like he was born in it. Oh, how I wanted to peel it off him. The man was a few inches over six feet with light brown hair and light eyes. The way those eyes bore into my soul had me ready to call the lawyer and tell him I was keeping the club. I wanted to slide Luke's jacket off his arms and rip his shirt open so I could see what the clothes were hiding. I'd never been as attracted to anyone as I was him. Not even Blake, who I'd spent the last four years with. I shouldn't even be thinking about Luke in such a way. If he was to be my employee, I would need to keep things professional between us, but that didn't stop my mind from going where it shouldn't.

When I realized I was still holding his hand while I

checked him out, I couldn't help but blush. I had to get myself together. If he was my manager, we would be working closely together, and I couldn't have him suing me for sexual harassment before I had the chance to even get my bearings. Dropping his hand, I didn't apologize. "It's a pleasure to meet you, Luke."

"My deepest condolences. Doug was a good man." Luke shoved his hands in his pants pockets, pulling them taut across his legs and – holy mother of God. I had to look away before I made a fool of myself.

Pretending it was his comment and not something else that had me flustered, I said, "Doug was a stranger to me. He left when I was six, and I haven't seen him since. You obviously knew a different Doug Caan than I did."

Luke opened his mouth to respond, then closed it. His demeanor had changed from open and flirty to something akin to hurt. I've seen enough disappointment in my time to recognize it, and it was obvious my father had meant something to this man, so I did the mature thing. "I apologize for being insensitive to your feelings. I'm sorry for your loss."

"Thank you. Let's step inside and get out of the heat," he offered, pulling a set of keys out of his pocket.

I followed him inside and paused to look around. I expected blood on the wooden floor and evidence of the crime scene unit having done their job with numbered markers and a chalk outline. I found nothing but a pristine setting. It was surreal seeing images of the woman I was named after adorning the walls. Dinah Washington, along with Billie Holliday, Ella Fitzgerald, and even Nina Simone held court, overlooking the place where my father spent most of his time. I wish I could say I possessed even an ounce of the talent my namesake did, but my only musical inclination was singing in the shower. Whatever. I had more important things to worry about like what the hell I was going to do with a jazz club in New Orleans.

"I took the liberty of calling in a cleaning crew. I didn't want you to see the place in disarray. In all honestly, I could have opened the club a couple nights ago, but I didn't want to step on any toes." Luke moved behind the bar and poured himself a drink. "Can I get you anything?" he asked, as if he owned the place. Being the manager for the last eight years earned him the right to feel at home. I was the one who was out of place, and my demeanor probably showed it.

"I'll have water, please." I needed to keep a level head. Not about being the new owner; that would come in time. Taking the proffered water, I sat across from Luke on one of the stools and wrapped my hands around the glass. "I have no knowledge of running an establishment such as this. I earned a degree in business, but I currently work in marketing for a major music producer."

"Please don't worry about the day-to-day operations. I've been overseeing The Limelight for almost a decade, and unless you have someone in mind to take my place, I would love to continue in that capacity." Luke silently studied me to the point I wanted to run out the door, hop on a plane, and return to Tennessee. When he spoke, his voice seemed to vibrate around the room. "You should sell the bar to me."

More goosebumps rose on my skin. I mentally shook off the weird vibe. "I would like to take some time and think about that."

Luke studied me intently. "I have put together several documents, which outline my roll and compensation within the organization as well as all the other employees. I've also included a document listing weekly costs versus revenue." He produced a ledger from behind the bar and placed it in front of me which I found odd. Everything was done electronically these days.

This was what I'd flown to Louisiana for. I was here on a fact-finding mission. Once I gathered a little intel, I was going back home and decide whether to uproot my life. If I decided to keep the bar, I would work with Luke to ensure things ran smoothly. I opened the folder and glanced over the contents. I would need a bit of time to study what Luke had prepared, but if the spreadsheet was accurate, The Limelight was running well in the black each week.

"Please feel free to reopen as soon as possible. I'll want to take a more thorough look at what you've prepared, but I don't see the need to change anything with regards to how the club is managed. I appreciate the ledger, but I'd like an electronic version as well."

"I will open the club as soon as I contact all our employees, and if you give me your email address, I'll send you all the information you need to make a decision." I gave him my email, which he typed into his phone. "Now that business is out of the way, what do you say to dinner? I would love to show you around our city. Well, at least the French Quarter. We won't have time to see everything New Orleans has to offer, but…" Luke waited like a kid asking his parents for a puppy – hopeful yet expecting a solid no. My stomach fluttered at the thought of going on a date. But it wasn't a date. It was a manager offering to show the new owner he could be useful for more than running the club.

"I would love to go to dinner with you. I can meet you back here around six, if that's okay?"

"Six is perfect, but I'd like to pick you up at your

hotel, if you don't mind."

I probably shouldn't agree to him driving me, but he did know the area better. "I don't mind. I'm staying at Caesar's. Text me when you get there, and I'll meet you in the lobby." There were plenty of hotels in NOLA, but I did love to try my hand at blackjack whenever I got the chance, and staying at the casino hotel would allow me to do so without having to go far to find a game.

"It's a date." Luke blushed, and I couldn't help but grin. Gone was the confident man who looked so put together in his suit. I was looking forward to getting to know every aspect of my new employee. Packing the ledger into my bag, I slid off the stool and slid the strap across my chest. Without looking back, I let myself out into the thrum of tourists. I'd never been to New Orleans, but I'd heard about the city. More especially, the French Quarter. When I got the call earlier asking me to meet Luke at seven, I left the hotel and walked around, browsing shops, and stopping to listen to the musicians on the corners. The smell would take some getting used to as would the different types of people. Nashville had panhandlers and musicians who sat along the sidewalks, but they were nothing compared to those who made their home in the French Quarter, and in broad daylight, no less. I stopped in a local restaurant for supper and remained there until it was time for my

21

meeting.

Instead of fighting the crowds on Bourbon Street, I kept to the side roads which was probably stupid since I was alone and the streets weren't well-lit. I avoided eye contact with those who I passed, continuing at a decent clip. When I reached the corner at Chartres, a possum walked over my grave, as my momma used to say. My skin prickled with unease as though someone were watching me. I had read how this city was filled to the brim with mystical properties from voodoo to witchcraft to ghosts, but I had thought it was nothing more than marketing to entice curious tourists. Now I bought into the bizarre nature of my surroundings. Something or someone was making my skin crawl. I grabbed onto the strap of my messenger bag and found my feet. Getting to Canal Street with more pedestrians eased my fear, but only slightly. The feeling of being watched stayed with me until I stepped into the elevator at my hotel. I leaned against the paneled wall and shook out my hands. Maybe I wasn't cut out for living here.

The lift rose steadily, and I rushed through the doors as soon as they opened, hurrying to my room. Thankfully, the hallway was void of other patrons, or I'd have felt foolish. I found the keycard and slotted it into the reader. As soon as I was inside, I dropped my bag onto the king-sized bed and removed the ledger.

Kicking off my shoes, I settled on the small sofa and placed the book on my lap. Still spooked, I placed it beside me and rose to look out the window. Being that high up, I couldn't make out faces of the pedestrians below.

What was I looking for? Someone who was staring back? A stranger looking guilty for following me? I had been a single female walking alone in a city known for its high crime rate, which I now realized was stupid. I didn't do that in Nashville, so why the hell had I thought it wise to do so in NOLA? Moving to the minibar, I chose a bottle of vodka and dumped the contents into a rocks glass. I added some ice, swirling the alcohol to chill it before taking a sip. I preferred it mixed with sweat tea, but the dorm-sized fridge was empty of drinks, tea or otherwise. Someone knocked on my door, and I held my breath. Had I been followed upstairs without realizing it? Instead of crossing the room and looking through the peephole – yes, I had seen too many action movies – I called out, "Who is it?"

"Flower delivery for Dinah Caan."

There were only three people who knew I was in town – Luke, his assistant, and Mr. Fielding. I set the glass down and opened my messenger bag where I retrieved my wallet. I didn't have much cash, but I found a twenty. I did look through the security hole, and sure enough, an older man held a vase filled with roses. I opened the door and offered the money.

"A tip was added to the payment, but I thank you for the kind gesture." He held out the vase, and I took it, thanking him, then backed into the room, letting the door close behind me. I placed the flowers on the entertainment center and removed the small envelope from the plastic holder. On the front was my name and room number. I pulled out the insert, and handwritten were two words –

Until Tonight

First, how did Luke manage to get two dozen roses delivered so quickly? But more importantly, how did he know my room number? Maybe the florist had called ahead? I stared at the roses. In the four years Blake and I dated, he had bought me flowers once and that was on the first-year anniversary from when we met. He gifted me jewelry on my birthday, and those items had been diamonds. I wasn't a diamond-wearing woman. My birthstone was opal, but Blake had called it boring. I looked down at the opal ring on my index finger and twisted it. It seemed my choice of jewelry wasn't the only thing he found boring. When we broke up, he admitted it was because our sex life was too vanilla, and he needed to branch out. I didn't have to ask what that meant. Neither of us had broached moving in together, and I'd dodged a bullet there. Breaking up was hard enough without having to split a household.

I mentally shook myself out of the past. I had too much of my future to dwell on. Although I wasn't meeting Mr. Fielding until the next day to hear my father's will, I already knew what it said. I was the owner of The Limelight, my father's house, and all his assets. The attorney hadn't disclosed how much cash or investments I was entitled to, but I had researched housing in the Garden District, and that would be a nice chunk of change if I sold it. I had no idea how much a jazz club was worth. It had to be a lot, but what would I do with all that money? If my mom were still alive, I would share it with her. When I was younger, she made sure I had everything I needed plus the things I wanted. I never questioned where the money came from. She was a nurse, and I assumed she made a good wage. It wasn't until I was older and living on my own that I learned how much it cost for rent and utilities and food. She never mentioned my dad sending child support, but now that I knew his lifestyle before he was killed, maybe he sent her a monthly check. I would find out when I had access to his bank account.

That was a tomorrow problem. For now, I needed to

focus on getting through dinner with Luke. I glanced once more at the roses, then went to the bedroom and surveyed the clothes I had brought. What did one wear on a non-date with the hottest man in Louisiana?

CHAPTER THREE

Lukas

DOUG'S BEAUTIFUL HOME had been torn apart. The floor was covered in valuable antiques, which had been shattered. Priceless artwork had been torn from their frames and shredded. The furniture was in pieces. I was angry until I stepped into Doug's music room. Then I had to stop myself from running out of the house and ripping apart the first vamp I found. His album collection had been destroyed. His favorite saxophone was nothing more than mangled metal. My sharp nails elongated as I tipped my head back and roared. Whoever did this was going to suffer. Human, vamp, witch, it didn't matter. I would find them and render them apart one body part at a time.

I slid to my knees and picked up the sax, cradling it in my arms, the same way I had Doug while waiting for him to open his eyes after I turned him. I never understood why the human meant so much to me. As an Ancient, I had my brothers. I didn't get close to anyone else, but Doug had been different. He had also been my last progeny. Why would I create another when he was perfect? The first time I heard him play, he had been invited to a neighboring jazz café. I was walking down Bourbon Street when the most soulful music wafted along the air amid the noisy revelers, the whores offering their bodies, the buskers banging their own tunes, and the whistles from policemen attempting to tame the beasts. I ducked into the café and stood beside the door, mesmerized. Instead of returning to The Limelight, I remained planted as Doug played song after song. When his set was over, I made my way through the throng of partiers, gave him my business card, and told him to meet me down the street after his last set was over for the night. He found me behind the bar, and when he sat down, I asked his story. Sipping a vintage brandy, he said he was from Memphis, Tennessee, where he played at various clubs. I offered him a job and included one of my houses where he could live rent-free; that was how impressed I was.

Doug turned down my offer though. He had a loving woman and a young child back home. That night, a friendship was born from our mutual love of the greatest jazz artists alive and dead, and we kept in touch. The artists I hired were good, but Doug was phenomenal, so I decided to pay him a visit just so I could listen to him again. It was a decision that changed both our lives. The club where he was playing was in a rougher area of town, and there was a riot that night. In a barrage of bullets, several patrons were hit as well as two waitresses and Doug. In the melee, I grabbed my friend and hauled him out the back door, using my preternatural speed and glamour getting him to my hotel room undetected. As he was bleeding out, I made him an offer, and that night, my progeny was reborn.

Leaving his woman, Trina, and daughter behind had been harder for Doug than going through the change. I remained in Memphis with him while he got his blood thirst under control, then I rented a car, drove him back to New Orleans, and moved him into my home. I taught him the ways of our kind. I shielded him from those who thought they were better than the humans they fed from. I had rules in place for my coven. Only take as much blood needed to sustain them. If they killed a human, I killed them. It wasn't that I cared for humans. Not really, but I wouldn't risk anyone finding out about vampires. We had hidden in the shadows for millennia and would continue to do so as long as I was in charge.

Once Doug had his baser urges contained, he began playing at The Limelight, and soon, our club was packed nightly. Doug developed a fanbase of men and women who tried to catch his attention. With his dark hair and green eyes, the young man was a looker, but it was his talent with the horn that transfixed the masses. Hell, I was as mesmerized as the patrons I served at the bar. He was living his dream, but he did so without his woman and child. That was his one regret in agreeing to be turned. Instead of getting to say goodbye, he walked away without looking back. He couldn't force himself to call Trina, so he wrote her a letter. He couldn't admit to what happened that night of the riot, so he lied and said he was running from trouble. If I had been able to pass my gifts to him, he could have brought them along, but he couldn't explain to Trina how he could no longer eat human food or walk in the sunlight. Instead, Doug sent monthly checks to help raise Dinah.

Dinah. There was no way I would allow her to walk into her father's house – now her house – and see it in such disarray. Since my coven was large, I couldn't police the city alone, so I'd long ago formed a team of vamps to patrol in my stead, and I paid them an outrageous amount to remain loyal. It took a few years after I gained control from Constantine to weed out the worst of our kind, but once I had, trouble had been almost non-existent. Until eight days ago. I called Stefan, the captain of my security team, and told him what I needed. I then called Doug's attorney and compelled him to keep Dinah away from the house for the time being. My plan was to personally replace everything that had been destroyed. I couldn't replicate all the antiques or paintings, but I could move some of mine from storage. Even if the attorney had a list of all Doug's belongings, I could assure the replacements were equally as valuable. Since I didn't have enough time between now and my date with Dinah, I directed Stefan to begin moving my things the next morning where I could be there to oversee everything. I trusted Stefan, but I did not have faith that whomever destroyed Doug's possessions wouldn't be watching.

The team Stefan chose couldn't clear out the wreckage until the sun went down, so I locked up the house, planning to meet them back there after my date. I should call and reschedule, as I was in a prickly mood, but the need to see Dinah overrode my attitude. I drove Uptown to my largest house. It was a French two-story with over ninety-six hundred square feet and where I stayed when I needed to be alone. I had long ago purchased all the houses around mine, ensuring only vamps had access to those properties. I offered Doug one of them, but he opted for a place in the Garden Distract to be closer to the club.

Instead of pulling into the garage, I parked in the

circular driveway, then made my way to the second-floor balcony that overlooked a perfectly manicured courtyard. I poured a glass of brandy and sipped it while leaning against the railing. For too long, life had been perfect. I led my coven in a mostly peaceful existence among humans and whatever other creatures roamed the streets at night. I fed when I needed to which wasn't often. I fucked whenever I wanted, choosing humans since there was less drama that way. The last time I bedded a vamp, she assumed she would become my queen and caused dissention amongst the other females. I staked her to prove a point. It had been a while since I last had sex. That had to be why Dinah was so appealing. I needed to get close to her, but if whoever killed Doug somehow found out I fancied his daughter, would they target her too?

Until I moved to Louisiana, I hadn't met other supernaturals. I didn't know exactly what type of beings they were, but I recognized them as other. Had one of them found out about vamps? Did they somehow know I was king of my kind? If so, why go after Doug and not me? I didn't have a team of security guards flanking my every move. I was the deadliest, so it wasn't necessary. Maybe that was it. They couldn't kill me, so instead, they hurt me another way. Maybe the killer would return to The Limelight once it reopened. Speaking of which, I sent Arabella a text requesting she contact the employees and let them know they were needed the next day. Their schedules were set in stone, so there was no need to scramble to ensure we had the right people on the right day. I had personally called each one to tell them the news of Doug's demise while letting them know they would continue to be paid while the club was closed. The staff had been with us for years, and I didn't want them to even consider moving to a different job because of the unexpected time off.

As the shadow from the lowering sun crossed my lawn, I realized the time. Since I was meeting Dinah as Luke and not myself, I glamoured my clothes into something casual. I didn't expect her to have brought a nice dress for the type of restaurant I frequented. I also forewent my high-end sports car for something less conspicuous. I strode to the house next door where a nice four-door sedan was parked I strode to the house next door where I kept a nice four-door sedan to make it appear someone lived there.

I sent Dinah a text through the car's Bluetooth that I would escort her from her room to the car. When I pulled into the covered drop-off area, she was exiting the building. Stubborn female. She did allow me to get out and open her door. I gave her my best smile, one I only allowed when I was Luke. A club manager slash

33

bartender needed to put on a friendly façade.

When we were both seated, she gestured at her clothing. "I hope this is okay for where we're going. When I packed, I didn't expect to need a nice dress."

"You're perfect." I put the car in drive and headed away from the hotel. New Orleans had numerous restaurants near the heart of the city, but I opted for one on the outskirts of town. It was housed in a former pharmacy and was more intimate than most. "Do you like your job?"

Dinah glanced at me, but I kept my eyes on the road. "It keeps me busy. I've met many country music stars, but most often, I'm at a desk fielding phone calls and emails. It's not exactly where I imagined I would be when I was younger, but it pays the bills."

"That didn't answer my question. Do you enjoy it?"

"I don't hate it, but I had no idea what I wanted to do with my life when I was in college. I knew I didn't want to be a nurse like my mother, and my father didn't pass along his musical talent, so I opted for a business degree."

"And now that you're older? Have you thought of something which you might enjoy?"

"Not really. My life isn't bad, Luke."

"I wasn't implying it is. I'm of the opinion that most people get stuck and don't look further than what they have. Granted, there are those who are unable to rise above their situation, but most don't even try."

"Does that mean you always wanted to manage a jazz club? Was that your life's passion when you were younger?"

"My ambitions were not such that I wanted to rule the world, but I do love my job." *I just can't tell you what it is.* "I meet different people every night, and I get to listen to the best genre of music while doing so."

"I take it you and my father were close?"

"He was my best friend."

"Did he…" Dinah cleared her throat. "Did he find someone else? You know, a woman?"

"No. Your mother was the love of his life."

"Do you know why he abandoned us?" Dinah whispered.

Not able to bear the sadness in her tone, I reached over and grasped her left hand, threading our fingers. I was surprised I'd gone that long without touching her. Something in Dinah Caan called to me on a cellular level, and I needed her as much as my next drop of blood. "It wasn't by choice. Your father… Let's just say the night of the riot changed everything for Doug. If he had remained in Memphis, your life and that of your mother's would have been in danger."

"Then why didn't he explain that? Why up and

35

leave without a word to my mom?"

"It was safer for you both if he cut ties. I know that doesn't appease the heartache, but he felt it was easier that way. He couldn't remain in Memphis, nor could he return until it was safe." I squeezed Dinah's hand. "It was never safe."

"But he lived his life out in the open in New Orleans. He played at The Limelight every night where anyone could find him if they searched his name on the internet."

"True, but here he had protection."

"Not enough, obviously," she muttered, and that drove a metaphorical dagger deep into my heart, knowing she was right.

"He shouldn't have been alone, Dinah. I don't know what he was doing at the club after hours. Why he was there without his security team. He left at his usual time. I locked up behind all the staff and closed out the system. When I arrived the next morning, there was no indication anything was amiss until I found his body. I called the police, and together we went over every inch of the place. There was no evidence someone broke in, so we assume he met his killer willingly. There is a keypad on both front and back entrances. Doug entered his code at four fifty-three."

"Are there no security cameras?"

"There are, but both outside and interior cameras had been tampered with. Someone hacked the system so the feed shut down at precisely four fifty and came back online fifteen minutes later."

"Do you think whoever was after him in Memphis found him?"

"No. Those responsible for the riot were either arrested or killed that night. Those who went to jail never made it out."

I flipped the turn signal and eased into the parking lot of the restaurant. "Can we put aside talk of Doug's murder while we eat? I would like to get to know you better without such sadness tainting our meal."

"Yes, sorry. It's just a lot to take in."

"Believe me, I know." I unbuckled and exited the car. When I opened Dinah's door, I held out my hand. When our palms touched, I squeezed gently. I'd long ago learned to tamp down my strength. When she was on her feet, I studied her face. Eyes the color and shape of Doug's stared back. I wanted to taste her plump lips, but I refrained. As I moved her away from the car to close the door, my skin prickled. Something was close by. Wrapping my arm around her waist, I steered her toward the entrance while scanning the area. I should have put her back in the car and drove away, but how did I explain I had a bad feeling? We were several yards from the door when my phone rang.

"I apologize, but I need to take this. Please have the hostess seat you, and I'll be right in."

Dinah agreed, and I reached in my pocket for my phone. It stopped ringing, so I tapped the screen to see my assistant's name. I hit redial, but it rang several times before going to voicemail. What the hell? I tried a couple more times, but Arabella never answered. Maybe she had rung me by mistake. I pocketed my phone, but instead of going inside, I walked around the building. I could sense another vamp in the area, but that wasn't unusual. Not wanting to keep Dinah waiting further, I went inside.

CHAPTER FOUR

Dinah

I WAS ANNOYED at Luke for taking a call. It reminded me of Blake and how business always came first. Then again, Luke had promised to reopen the club at my request, so if his call had anything to do with that, I couldn't be upset. I stepped up to the small desk to the right as soon as I entered the building. The interior was quaint with lit sconces flickering against dark paneling. A bar sat along the wall to the left where several patrons were having a drink.

The hostess appeared from around the wall behind the desk. "Good evening. Just one?"

"No, my date is right behind me. He had to take a phone call."

"Would you like to wait or be seated?"

"Be seated, please."

The pretty woman pulled two menus from underneath the desk. "Right this way." I followed through the dining room and took the chair the hostess indicated. "Justine will be your server."

"Thank you." I opened the menu while I waited on Luke. He slid into the seat next to me a few minutes later. "Everything okay?"

Luke smiled, but it didn't reach his eyes. "I'm not sure. My assistant called but hung up before I could answer. When I dialed her back, it went to voicemail. I'll worry about her later."

The server stepped up to our table. "Good evening. My name is Justine... Oh, hello, Mr. Bennett. What can I get you to drink?"

Luke gestured for me to go first. "I'll have a gin and tonic with extra lime."

"I'll have my usual," Luke ordered without looking at her.

"Coming right up." Justine didn't linger.

I smirked at Luke when he glanced my way. "So, Mr. Benett, I take it you come here often?"

Luke still seemed tense, so unlike the man I'd met earlier. "Often enough. Did you have a chance to look at the menu?"

"Not really." I perused the dinner offerings, which were several steps up from jambalaya and crawfish étouffée. Some of it I'd never heard of, so I chose a red snapper and crab plate. By the time I decided, Justine was back with our drinks.

"Would you care for an appetizer?" she asked, not looking at Luke.

"None for me. It'll spoil my main course. Luke?"

He declined, and we both ordered. I got the snapper, and he ordered the pithivier. It was one of the dishes I didn't recognize, so I would be able to see what it was without asking. Justine took our menus, and I picked up my gin, holding it out toward Luke. He raised his Scotch, and I toasted, "To the beginning of a new partnership." We clanked our glasses and each took a sip.

"Partnership, huh?" Luke asked, his head tilted. He scanned the restaurant before bringing his eyes back to me. He was clearly distracted.

"Yes. I'm counting on you to continue managing the club. From what I saw of the numbers, you're quite good at it."

Luke set his glass down but kept his long fingers wrapped around it. "I'll be honest with you, Dinah. Your father was the reason the club did so well. He was a gifted musician, and he had a large following. Nobody can replace him, but we will need to hire someone to play each night. It is a jazz club, after all." Luke lifted his glass, but it froze in front of his face as he looked around. A man just as handsome as Luke appeared out of nowhere and took the seat next to me.

"Pardon the interruption," he said.

Luke straightened in his seat, placing his glass on the table with a thunk. "What are you doing here, Laurent?"

Laurent focused on me. His eyes were lavender, so I assumed he wore contacts. He stared at me with the same intensity Luke had when I first met him. Laurent leaned closer. "You will remember nothing of this conversation."

What an odd thing to say. The air around us felt heavy, the way it had when Luke said I should sell him the club.

Laurent stared at me a beat before turning his gaze to Luke. He lowered his voice to barely a whisper. "You have a problem, Brother."

"We've already established that, but why are you in my territory?"

Brother? Territory? I picked up my drink and took a sip, avoiding either man's eyes.

Laurent leaned back and angled toward Luke. "I'm here because I had a visit from Edward."

"What's he doing in the States?" Luke asked.

"He came to warn me." Since Laurent was under the assumption I wouldn't remember this conversation, I kept my gaze locked on a painting across the room. He didn't continue speaking because Justine took that moment to deliver our food.

"Oh, I didn't realize you had a third person. What can I get you to drink, Sir?"

"A double of your most expensive bourbon, neat."

"Would you like a menu as well?" she asked.

"No, thank you."

Justine gestured to our plates. "Can I get you anything else?"

"We're all set, Justine. Thank you," Luke responded, but I asked for another drink. I had a feeling I was going to need it. Once she was across the room, Luke asked, "Warn you about what?" Luke didn't touch his food, and when he noticed me not eating, he said, "You should eat, Dinah."

I nodded wordlessly and picked up my fork. I was no longer hungry, but I couldn't let on that this conversation bothered me.

Laurent drummed his fingers on the table as Justine returned with his drink. "Thank you." He took a sip, waiting for her to retreat. "Did you know Lillith created more of us?"

Created? What the actual hell? I almost choked on my bite of fish.

"No, I didn't. When did this happen?"

"According to Edward, about forty years ago.

43

They're spread out in the western part of the world. Or at least they were, hence, your problem."

"Are you telling me a new Ancient is here? Why didn't you call me?"

"And have someone eavesdrop on our conversation? You know better, Lukas. I made sure there were none of your coven here before I sat down. I couldn't even trust a letter not to fall into the wrong hands. Neither could Edward. These new Ancients are ruthless. They aren't satisfied with what Lillith gave them. Edward took one out about six months ago. Before going after Edward, Titus, the new bastard, killed Elizabeth."

Luke grabbed my free hand. "How is he even functioning?"

Laurent noticed the gesture. Arching a brow, he asked, "Something you want to tell me, Brother?"

Luke jerked his hand back as though he'd been burned. "No. She's just the new owner of the club. Nothing more."

Well hell. Call me all kinds of a fool, but I thought the flowers meant something. That this date meant he was interested.

Laurent continued. "Edward loved Elizabeth, but she wasn't his beloved. Still, he is now ruled by vengeance. Before Edward took Titus's head, he

44

compelled him to spill where other newbies are ruling. They're spread out in Africa and Asia for the most part, but Titus said a few were coming after our territories. After he met with me, Edward sharpened his sword and set out for South Africa."

"How do you know one is in my territory?"

"I don't, but after what happened to Doug, I assumed it was an Ancient because one of your coven wouldn't risk your wrath. Would they?"

Luke rubbed his temples. When he looked up, his eyes were the same odd lavender color of Laurent's. I gasped, unable to stop myself.

"Are you okay?" Luke asked.

"Please excuse me. I need to use the restroom." I grabbed my purse and stood before he could stop me. I passed Jasmine who had my fresh drink. I took it from her, drank it all down, then placed the empty on the tray. I continued to the back of the restaurant where the bathrooms were. I sequestered myself in one of the stalls and sat down on the toilet. I attempted to make sense of the conversation, but I couldn't. I also couldn't stay there. I needed distance between myself and… Hell, I couldn't comprehend what Luke and Laurent could possibly be if they were created. I pulled out my phone and ordered a ride. There was a car nearby, less than two minutes away, so I exited the bathroom, checking the hallway to ensure Luke hadn't followed. When the coast was clear, I found the back door. Nobody stopped me, so I pushed it open and stepped out into the muggy air, running into a hard body.

"Excuse me," I apologized.

"Hello, Dinah."

I snapped my head up at my name. Like Luke and Laurent, this man was stunning. Unlike them, his eyes were an eerie red, and his canines extended in ominous points. It was almost Halloween, and I wondered if he was in costume. If he was, it was a good one, but vampires weren't real. When I tried to step around him, he reached for me, his nails digging into my upper arms. I dropped my purse in an effort to fight him off, but he was too strong. Tossing me over his shoulder as though I weighed nothing, he took off running with a strong arm banded around my thighs.

"Luke!" I tried to call out, but it was nothing more than a croak. The beast, because this was no human, moved with a speed that was incomprehensible. Normally, I wasn't the type to get queasy, but hanging upside down wasn't doing me any favors. Neither was the ground that was nothing more than a blur.

"Dinah!" Luke yelled, although it sounded farther away than it should. How far had the beast run? Were there not people on the sidewalks witnessing my

46

abduction? None of this made sense. Maybe I was back at the hotel, having fallen asleep, and in the midst of a nightmare. Would it be considered a nightmare during the day? A daymare? Shit, I was losing my mind.

When the beast finally stopped, he dropped me to the ground. I barely resisted the bile threatening to spew forth as I landed hard on my ass. "She's all yours," he said to someone.

A female squatted in front of me a few feet away, studying me like a specimen under a microscope. "I should have kept your father alive long enough to see what happens next."

"You killed my father?"

"Sure did. Bastard was a sucker for a pretty face. Then again, so am I." She cupped my cheeks in her hands and leaned forward, pressing her lips to mine. I was so stunned that I didn't register the pain in my neck until she moved back, studying her hand. Long claws dripped with blood which she licked. "Mmm. You taste so sweet. Too bad Lukas won't get here in time to save you. He'll fail you just as he failed your father." She stood, flipping her blonde hair over her shoulder.

I was already dizzy from the zooming, but now I felt as though I were going to pass out. My neck throbbed, and when I grabbed it, it was wet. I pulled my hand away, and it was coated in blood. I wasn't going to faint;

I was dying.

"Why?" I managed to ask.

"To send a message. Lukas Benoit is weak. He leads peacefully, and that's not what we were created to do." She put a finger to my forehead and pushed. I fell backwards, gasping for air. As darkness overtook me, I thought I should have stayed in Nashville.

My body was on fire with need, and my throat was parched. I reached up to rub it and flinched when I scratched myself. I jerked my hand away, and that's when I saw them. Sharp claws like the ones on the man who'd grabbed me. Then I remembered the woman's hand. She had sliced my throat, and I died. Didn't I? Was this my version of Hell? I never gave much thought to the afterlife before. I lived the way my mom taught me, being kind and giving when I could. Maybe I hadn't been good enough. I squinted against the harsh light and saw I was in a bedroom. Did Hell have bedrooms? I didn't think so, but what did I know?

That same woman was talking nearby. Her words were so clear she could have been a foot away from me. "It's done. I'm just waiting on her to wake up, which should take about another hour. Then I'm going to let her loose on the city. She'll be delirious since I didn't give her enough blood to keep her from turning feral. Lukas will have to come for her when she rips through

48

the humans to sate her thirst. While he's preoccupied, I'll take his head."

Vampires were real? And this bitch – the one who'd killed my father – had turned me into one? No. No, no, no! I rolled off the bed, steadying myself with a hand on the dresser. I glanced at the mirror and cringed. I looked like a wild version of myself. One with fangs. My eyes were light purple, the same as Luke's had been for a moment at the restaurant. I didn't want fucking fangs. I didn't want to be a monster. I stumbled to the door, threw it open, and rushed from the room, slamming into the opposite wall. Whoa. Too fast.

"It seems she's awake. I'll call you back," the woman told whoever she was talking to. Before she had a chance to come upstairs, I rushed down them, slamming into her.

"What did you do to me?" I yelled, reaching out with clawed hands.

"Control yourself, Dinah."

"Don't tell me to control myself!" I slashed out, but she slapped my hand away.

"You were dying, so I remade you into something better. Stronger. Would you rather I let you perish?"

"I was dying because you fucking slashed my throat, you bitch." My chest was heaving, and my fangs bit into my bottom lip as I spoke.

"Now, now. No need for name calling. And yes, I slashed your throat. It had to be done, you see. I bet you're thirsty."

She wasn't wrong. My throat was still on fire, and my fangs ached to latch onto her neck.

"I'll take you somewhere to get a drink. How does that sound?"

That sounded awful and wonderful in equal measure. I needed to quench my thirst, but if I did, that would bring Luke to her. I had to protect him. She said I would be delirious. I wasn't. I was pissed at being turned and used as her plaything. How did one pretend to be delirious? I stumbled as I searched the room for something I could use against her. Did it matter that I was a... what was it Laurent called the freshly made vampires? Newbies? Wait. He also mentioned someone called an Ancient. Was this woman one of those? If so, was I strong enough to take her out? She needed a distraction to kill Luke, so maybe that's what I needed as well. I turned in circles, waving my arms like a lunatic. In one of my rotations, I spotted a sword. Was that how she planned on killing Luke? Not on my fucking watch. I had only known him a short while, but he was special, not just because he was the leader of his coven. No, he meant something to me.

"Dinah, stop spinning. It'll be okay, I promise. You

just need to come with me, and I'll teach you everything you need to know."

"So thirsty," I rasped. I wasn't lying. I made a dash for the kitchen and turned on the faucet. I dipped down and drank.

She followed with a huff. "That's not going to quench your thirst, I'm afraid. You need blood."

I raised up, water dripping down my chin. "Blood, yes. Give me yours." I rushed her, but she was too fast. She grabbed my arms, shaking me so hard that my teeth rattled. I really hated this bitch.

"No, Dinah. I can't give you any more. We need to hunt. Come with me." With an iron grip on my arm, she dragged me toward the door, the sword just out of reach. I knew she was lying, but she was stronger, so I needed to come up with plan B.

CHAPTER FIVE

Lukas

I STARED OFF after Dinah. She grabbed her fresh drink from Justine's tray and drank it all down before continuing to the bathroom. I had no problem with a woman who could hold her liquor, but her vibe had been all wrong when she rose from the table.

Laurent swirled the amber liquor in his glass. "You know, Brother, there's nothing wrong with taking a queen."

"And have her end up like Elizabeth? No, thank you. I've already lost her father. I won't put Dinah in harm's way." Of all the other Ancients – my brothers – I was closest with Laurent. He and I were most alike and chose territories relatively close. Where I ruled the southeast, Laurent's area was the southwest region of the US.

"She's Doug's daughter?" I nodded, and he sighed. "She's already at risk by being seen with you. Thank

Lillith I compelled her to forget our conversation, or she might have been hurt at your dismissal of your feelings."

"There are no feelings," I lied.

Laurent shook his head. "You can lie to yourself, but I know you. You wouldn't have gotten so close to Doug if you didn't crave a partner."

My fangs extended before I could stop them, and someone shrieked. I waved a hand the waitress's direction, and said, "You saw a Halloween costume." Dazed, she walked away. Dazed... "Holy goddess, Dinah's eyes. Laurent, I'm not sure she was compelled. Fuck, I totally forget. When we were at the club, I compelled her to sell the place to me, and she said she would need to think it over instead of agreeing."

"If that's the case, she knows too much. You have to remake her. Or end her permanently."

"No!" I took a deep breath. "No. I want her, but I will not risk her. Not while there's an unknown killer in my territory."

"Like I said, she's already at risk. All you can do is keep her with you at all times until the threat is neutralized."

I downed my drink as I waited for Dinah to return from the restroom. My skin prickled, and I set the glass down. "There's someone close. Do you feel it?"

53

"Yes. I'll pay the tab while you—" Laurent and I froze as a several of my coven ran into the restaurant. Before I knew what was happening, they started attacking the humans. Those who weren't being targeted screamed and scrambled toward the door.

Fuck! "Stop!" I commanded both humans and vamps. The humans froze before they could get outside. The vamps turned their red eyes my way, blood dropping down their faces. I stalked to the nearest one. "What the fuck are you doing?"

"Feeding."

"In a fucking public restaurant?"

"He told us to."

"Who told you to?"

"Scary vamp. Didn't get his name."

Laurent fisted his hands. "This is a diversion. Go get your female. I'll handle this."

I ran to the back where the restrooms were located, and I knocked on the door. Pushing it open a crack, I called her name. "Dinah? Is everything okay?" When she didn't answer, I entered the small room, but it was empty. Since she hadn't returned to the front of the restaurant, I found the back door and exited the building. The air was filled with scents I recognized, and Dinah's was the most prominent. Her purse was on the ground. While I had been distracted, someone had taken my female. My fangs dropped as I roared, "Dinah!"

I had no idea which way she'd been taken, but that didn't stop me from trying to find her. I used my advanced sight to search for anything amiss. I sped back and forth in every direction, coming up empty. With each mile I went my anger rose. Eventually, I gave up, returning to the restaurant. I stormed inside.

"She's not here. They fucking took her while that — " I gestured at my coven members who hadn't moved, " — was happening."

Laurent was standing court over the vamps. "I've compelled the humans, but you need to deal with your coven. While you do that, I'll search for the Ancient."

"What about your own territory?"

He shrugged. "My second has everything handled. Unless he calls and says something is going on there, I'm here for you, Lukas."

I gave Laurent a key to my house, then he left me to deal with the aftermath of what my vamps had done. I didn't care that they'd been compelled by an Ancient. I approached the one I'd spoken to, shoved my hand into his chest, and pulled out his heart. He and the organ turned to ash. I ended each vampire. Thankfully, I had stopped them before they killed any humans. Compelling a full restaurant wasn't hard, but it still pissed me off that I needed to. I made sure that those who had been fed from healed. I instructed Justine and one of the other servers to vacuum up the ashes while I gathered the vamps' clothes and took them out to my car. I approached the manager and had him erase the security feed for the entire evening. When the restaurant was free from any evidence of what happened, I instructed them to return to their meals.

Stepping outside, I breathed deeply. I needed to rip someone apart. This stranger had taken everything from me that meant something. First Doug and now Dinah. I'd had so little time with her, and now I wouldn't get to know her. I wouldn't get to find out if she could return my feelings. I wouldn't stop searching until I retrieved her body so I could give her a proper burial. My phone vibrated, and when I saw Stefan's name, I remembered I was supposed to meet the crew at Doug's house. Cleaning it up for Dinah was now a moot point, but it would give me something to do to take my mind off killing newly made Ancients.

I answered the phone and filled Stefan in on what happened with Dinah. I couldn't tell him about Ancients, but I did tell him there was someone in my territory who shouldn't be there. I tasked him with putting together more vamps to keep their eyes and ears on the pulse in the city since I couldn't be everywhere at once. I asked that the cleanup crew meet me at Doug's in half an hour. I made my way across town to the Garden District. With as many abled bodies as Stefan sent, the house was cleared out before midnight. It was no longer necessary to replace all the things that had been destroyed, but for some reason, I felt the need to put the house back the way it had been. I had accumulated a wealth of antiques and artwork over the years, and it would be better suited to adorn Doug's house than to sit in storage.

I was still seething by the time the crew left. Two of Stefan's team remained to keep watch in case the culprit decided to return, so I got in my car and drove around the city searching for a blood donor. I could go months without feeding, but as irate as I was, if I drank from a human in the mood I was in, I might take too much. Or worse. I stopped at one of my houses in the Quarter where I had bags of blood stored. I sucked down four pints of A positive, then grabbed a bottle of my favorite Scotch, taking it to the rooftop garden. I plopped down on one of the padded lounge chairs, took a long pull from the bottle, then stared at the moon. I didn't understand why I was being targeted. I had ruled my area for centuries with no issues. My coven was happy. If they weren't, I would have known. I paid Stefan's team well to keep me apprised of anyone who was disgruntled. Anyone who needed help in living during the nighttime hours. Sure, there were those who felt that humans should be fair game with no consequence, but I compelled them to see things my way.

If what Laurent said about the new Ancients was true, it was possible they disagreed with how I oversaw my territory. What better way to take my attention away from my coven than to kill those who meant the most to me? But how did they know that? I spent time at Doug's house, and he visited mine, something I didn't do with other coven members. Someone would have had to watch my coming and going for months though. If it was an Ancient, that would be easy enough since they could glamour themselves and I'd be none the wiser since I didn't know what they looked like, and we were able to shield our power from others. Hell, they wouldn't have to mask their true visage. They could have sat in The Limelight, cloaked as a regular patron. I didn't pay attention to those who came to the club that weren't regulars because we got so many tourists. They could have walked the sidewalk in front of Doug's house after following me from mine.

I swallowed half the bottle, then wiped my mouth with the back of my hand. If I were anyone else, I might pack up and move to a new territory, but this was my city, dammit. I loved New Orleans. I loved the culture. The mystical properties. The history. The kids who busked on street corners. No, I wouldn't let some pissant baby Ancient run me off. I polished off the rest of the Scotch and placed the bottle on the floor, then closed my eyes, letting myself wallow in the loss of not getting more time with Dinah.

Glass breaking downstairs roused me from my nap. Fuck, my sword was at the main house where Laurent was. If I survived the night, I would put one in every house I owned. I eased off the chaise lounge and crept toward the door. Someone was downstairs, and they weren't being quiet. I eased the door closed behind me as a light came on.

"Fuck," whoever was down there cursed, and the light went out again. Something scraped across the floor, then a softer light cast a shadow over the landing outside the kitchen. "Yes," they rasped, and then a soft moan followed. What in Lillith's name was going on? I padded down the steps on silent feet. I could have used my supernatural speed to surprise them, but I didn't want to startle whoever it was in case they were an Ancient. Then again, if they were an Ancient, they already knew I was close by.

When I hit the bottom step, I held my breath and peered quickly around the corner. An extremely disheveled female stood with the refrigerator door open and was tearing into a bag of blood. Wait. I would know

59

those curves anywhere. Oh, thank Lillith, but how was she here?

"Dinah?"

She turned with a hiss, blood seeping down the sides of her mouth. Her hair was wild, and her eyes were the same lavender as mine when I wasn't using glamour. I held up my hands to show her I meant no harm. As a newly turned vamp, she would be strong and unpredictable.

"Sweetheart?"

"So thirsty." Dinah tossed the empty on the floor and snagged another from the still open fridge. Puncturing the bag with her fangs, she drank deeply.

"I'm thrilled to see you, Sweetheart. Can you tell me what happened?"

"Thirsty."

"Yes, I'm sure you are, but I need to know who did this to you."

"Blonde bitch. Hates you."

That could be any number of female vamps in my coven. "Does this blonde bitch have a name?" My phone rang, but I ignored it.

Dinah shrugged and tossed the bag down with the first one. She grabbed one more, but this one, she sipped more slowly. I wanted to rush to her and take her in my arms, but I wasn't sure how that would be received, so I waited her out. Thinking of the timeline, she couldn't have been awakened from her death very long. Whoever turned her must not have taken good care of her, but why would they? And how did she get away from them?

"How did you find me?"

Dinah tapped her chest. "In here." When she finished her third bag, she dropped it, then wiped her mouth with the collar of her blood-stained blouse. Before I knew what was happening, she crossed the room, grabbed my shirt with both hands, and slammed her mouth to mine. I jerked back. "Mindful of the fangs, Sweetheart."

"Fuck. I forgot about those." Her fangs disappeared into her gums, and I stared at her in amazement.

"How did you do that?" It took newbies a long time to get their fangs and claws under control, but Dinah retracted hers easily.

She tilted her head to the side. "Just thought they needed to go back into hiding. Can I kiss you now? Or is blood breath a thing?"

I couldn't help but grin. "Considering I'm a vampire, I couldn't care less about blood breath. And as much as I would love to kiss you, we need to talk." And yes, I was an idiot for stopping my vixen from kissing me, but this shit was important. Once I figured out who the blonde bitch was and dispensed of her, there would be kissing and so much more.

"No," she whined. "Those four words are the kiss of death. Well, I guess there's another type of kiss that can kill you. One with fangs."

"Who kissed you?" I growled.

"The blonde bitch. Said my father was a sucker for a pretty face and so was she." And now I had more reason to end this woman.

"Sweetheart, how did you get away from her?"

"She turned me loose, expecting me to hunt. I found you instead."

"But how? You should be wild with need, feeding from anyone you could. Did you feed on humans, Sweetheart?" Nothing about this made sense. There was no way Dinah could ignore the humans in the area.

"No. I didn't want to kill an innocent by accident. I overheard her on the phone saying that she didn't give me enough blood to keep me from going feral, but she must have miscalculated. I wasn't delirious, I only pretended to be. Then she took me to a park and turned me loose."

"You said you found me in here." I placed my fingers above her heart.

"Yeah. It was like a game of hot or cold; you know where you have to figure out something and the person

62

who knows the answer tells you if you're getting hotter or colder? I could feel your... I guess your spirit? Your heartbeat? Something led me here to you. But when I got to the house, I could smell the blood in the fridge, so I helped myself. I hope that's okay. And sorry about the window. I'll pay to have it fixed."

There was no way... She felt me? Holy Lillith. I never expected to find my beloved, but if she located me using our bond, there was no other explanation. I slid my hand up her neck and carded my fingers through her ratty hair, then pressed our lips together. Dinah opened her mouth, her tongue finding mine. She wrapped her strong arms around my neck and deepened the kiss. In all my years, I had never experienced such a connection from a kiss. Not even sex had been this explosive. But it wouldn't have been because none of the others had been my beloved. I didn't know how it was possible since I wasn't the one who turned her, but then again, I wasn't that well-versed in regards to the one being designed for me. As far as I knew, only one of my brothers had found his, and he'd turned her himself.

When we came up for air, I pressed my forehead to hers. "I'm not worried about the window. I am worried that this woman may have followed you."

Dinah stiffened in my arms. "Shit, I forgot. She

planned to use me as a distraction."

"And it worked like a charm," a familiar voice said as they entered the house.

I turned, pushing Dinah behind me, to find Constantine's former second. "Darius." I was surprised he would risk coming back into my territory after I banished him.

Darius swung a sword in a figure eight. "Surprise. Although I do have to say, the surprise is on me. Dinah, how did you find your way to Lukas? You should have killed twenty humans between the park and here with your hunger."

Dinah lunged for Darius, but I grabbed her around the waist. "Easy."

Darius smirked, but there was also uncertainty in his eyes. Dinah's strength was a wild card, one Darius hadn't planned on.

"He's the one who abducted me," Dinah seethed. Another reason to end him permanently.

"Who are you working with?" I asked, doubting he would give up their name.

"What makes you think I'm working with someone?" He slid his finger along the edge of the blade, drawing blood.

"Because you didn't turn me. That crazy blonde bitch did. I heard her on the phone making your plan,"

Dinah admitted, ignoring the fresh blood available a few feet away.

When she didn't take the bait, Darius licked his finger, eyeing Dinah. He had to be confused as to why Dinah wasn't out of her mind with hunger. I had to admit I was too, but the only thing that made sense was the fact that she was my beloved, and that gave her strength and willpower she wouldn't normally have. How much? I wasn't sure. And that was what kept me from turning her loose.

"Let's just say I'm not the only one tired of hiding my true nature. You should have left Constantine in charge. He knew vamps are the superior species."

"We may be stronger and faster, but if humans found out about us, it would be chaos. Vamps are grossly outnumbered."

"So what? Lillith created us to wreak havoc, not hide from the world. She grew tired of seeing her first Ancients cower, so she made a new batch. Ones who have the balls to be what we were meant to be."

Fuck, the Ancient had shared what we are. That explained why a made vamp had a sword. "Did Lillith mention that her first Ancients are also stronger? That we're brothers who have each other's back?"

"And where are your brothers now?"

"Here." Laurent strode into the room, his face a dark

storm.

Darius swirled, raising his sword at the last second, but Laurent was already swinging his. He knocked the weapon out of Darius's hand, and the bastard dove for it, but Dinah got there first. Darius clawed at Dinah's back and arm, and that infuriated me. No one touched my beloved and lived. With his attention elsewhere, I grabbed the vamp by the head, pulling him away from Dinah. The male went wild, but he was no match for my strength. I twisted his head, severing his spinal cord, and dropped him to the floor. Dinah, who was now on her feet, raised the sword and drove it into his chest. Within seconds, Darius's body turned to ash.

CHAPTER SIX

Dinah

I PUSHED MY wild hair off my face, stalked over to Luke, and threw my arms around his waist, resting my head on his chest. He snuggled me tight as he said, "Thank you, Brother. How are you here?"

"The two males you had guarding Doug's house didn't report in on time, and when Stefan couldn't get ahold of them, he went to Doug's and found them dead. He tried calling to warn you, and when you didn't answer, he came to the house. Since you weren't there, he called all the vamps he had patrolling the city to find your car. When it was reported you were here, Stefan pulled up a map and showed me where this house was located. I grabbed my sword and ran like the wind."

"You have my gratitude."

Laurent waved him off. "Now what? We still don't know who he was working for."

"Maybe if we find the female who turned Dinah, we

can find the Ancient."

Laurent pointed at me. "She knows?"

"Not everything, but I will tell her in due time."

I turned loose and squatted next to the pile of ashes and sifted through it until I found Darius's phone. I tapped the screen, frowning at it. "I don't know his passcode."

"Whoever he was working with will eventually call. How about I man the phone while you get cleaned up?" Laurent suggested to me.

"Fine, but I need more blood. I'm thirsty again."

"I'll feed you, Sweetheart. And once you've had a chance to clean up, we'll head to one of my other houses to regroup."

"One of… Are you rich or something?"

"You could say that."

"But you're a manager of a club."

Luke sighed. "I have much to tell you, but first, let's get you in the shower." Without asking, he lifted me easily and carried me to a large en suite, then set me on my feet. I caught my reflection in the mirror and sighed. I looked worse than I had when I first woke up. Luke wrapped his arms around me from behind, nestling his face in the crook of my shoulder.

"She said you would fail me like you failed my father. Were you too late? Were you going to make him a vampire?"

Luke raised his head, staring at my reflection. "Why don't I feed you while I tell you a story?" He extended one of his claws, sliced his forearm, and pressed it to my mouth. As soon as the scent of his blood hit my nose, I dove at his arm, gnawing at it with sharp teeth. His blood called to me, and I answered, drinking it down as fast as I could.

"Easy, Sweetheart. I know you're thirsty, but you need to pace yourself."

I did as he suggested as the most delicious flavor burst across my tongue and down my throat. Luke's blood was a hundred times better than that bagged stuff.

"I turned Doug the night of the riot. He was caught in the crossfire, and when I got to him, he was bleeding out. I couldn't let him die, so I turned him, then brought him back to New Orleans once he had his blood craze under control enough to travel that far."

I removed my fangs from his arm and licked the excess from my lips. "You walk around in the daylight. How is that possible?" I sounded funny, raspy, talking around fangs, so I recalled them. I wasn't sure I'd ever get used to the feel of them sliding back into my gums.

Luke reached in the large shower and turned on the water. "Because I'm an Ancient. That means I was created by Lillith, the goddess of the underworld. The

69

rules for vampires turned by other vamps don't apply to me. I can consume human food and drink. Go out in the sunlight. I don't need blood as often as someone freshly turned."

When I was sated, I kept hold of the wrist I had drank from. There was no sign of where he slashed his arm or where I'd dug my teeth into his skin. "Did I hurt you?" I asked.

"No, Sweetheart. You can't hurt me. Not physically, anyway."

"You think I would hurt you emotionally?"

"Only if you don't return my feelings."

"But at the restaurant, you told Laurent I was nothing more than the owner of the club. Your words cut me deep. It's why I excused myself to the restroom. I had to get out of there before I made a bigger fool of myself."

"Old habits die hard. If anyone knew what you meant to me, they would use you as a pawn, the way they did your father. Then again, they used you anyway. Compulsion doesn't work on you. That should have clued me in that you were more special than I imagined. I tried it at the club when I told you that you should sell the club to me. And then Laurent compelled you to forget our conversation, only it didn't work." Luke cupped my cheeks in his hands. "Dinah, I felt drawn to you the first moment I spotted you outside The Limelight. And now I know why. You are my beloved, the one creature specifically chosen to be mine."

"That's the reason I was able to find you."

"Yes."

"And if I told you I wanted to peel your suit off you the second I laid eyes on you?"

"I'd say you're welcome to get me naked anytime you wish." Luke unbuttoned the ruined blouse. I normally would have asked to shower alone, but who the hell was I kidding? I'd wanted to strip him bare the first time I saw him. His eyes darkened the more skin was revealed. His fangs extended, and I shivered. "Are you going to bite me?"

"If you'll let me. You've had my blood, and although I am dying to taste yours, we do need to change locations. But I promise you this, as soon as the threat is over, you and I are going to spend days getting to know one another, both in and out of bed." His fangs receded, and he took a step back. "Let's get cleaned up, shall we?" He removed his clothes before I could blink. When I got a look at all his fair skin, I froze. How utterly perfect was this man? "Pants, Sweetheart."

"Oh, yeah." I finished undressing and joined him under the water. Luke took care, washing every inch of my skin before shampooing my hair. There was no conditioner in the enclosure, but I would deal with the tangles later. I relished the feel of his fingers on my scalp. Every touch sent an aching need coursing through my body. I didn't know if it was a beloved thing or a Luke thing, but the cause didn't matter. It only mattered that I wanted him for an eternity.

Luke didn't have a brush so I detangled my hair the best I could with my fingers after towel-drying it. I had to borrow one of his T-shirts since my blouse was a mess. Thankfully, my pants and shoes were blood-free. Luke dressed in one of his expensive suits, and I wanted to rip it off his body. His eyes darkened again at seeing me in his clothes, but we didn't have time for horizontal shenanigans. We met Laurent downstairs who was standing by the door with his sword over his shoulder. He pointed to Darius's sword that was lying on the sofa. "I cleaned the blood off for you."

When I didn't move to take it, Luke picked it up, stepped back, and swung it in an arc. "It's a good blade. The perfect weight for you. I'll get you a sheath for it." He pulled a throw off the back of the sofa and wrapped it around the weapon before handing it to me.

"Shouldn't you keep it?"

"I have several."

"Well, then, thank you." I'd never held a sword before that night, but if we were going up against

Ancient vampires, it made sense for me to have one.

"If you'd like, I'll drive and you two can sit in the back in case Dinah needs to feed again."

Luke inclined his head. "I would appreciate that."

"Do we need to clean that up?" I asked, pointing at the ashes.

"I'll call one of my men," Luke said.

"How often will I need to feed?" I asked Luke as he passed the keys over to his brother.

"If you were a normal vamp, I would say every few hours the first day, then once a day for about a week. But you aren't normal. The fact that you bypassed every human you encountered until you reached me speaks volumes of your strength. And with me feeding you, it's possible you'll get your blood craze under control much sooner since mine is Ancient blood. It worked for your father."

Laurent narrowed his eyes. "You told her?"

"She is my beloved," Luke responded.

Laurent's face lit up, and he clapped Luke on the shoulder. "Congratulations, Lukas. This is amazing news."

"I agree," Luke murmured, cupping my face, and pressing his lips to mine.

"We need to go," Laurent said, interrupting our moment. He exited the house first, then told us it was clear. I wasn't used to this cloak and dagger stuff, but now that I knew what I meant to Luke, I would need to be on my guard. Once we were on our way, I asked Luke, "How big is your coven?"

"In New Orleans proper, around one hundred, but my territory extends farther than the city. I oversee close to three hundred vamps. Laurent has his own territory, as do other Ancients. There are some areas which are led by made vamps, but we leave them alone as long as they aren't killing humans and threatening our existence."

"How old are you? If that's okay to ask."

Laurent chuckled from the front seat. "We're called Ancients for a reason."

I stared at him in the rearview mirror. "So really old?"

Luke put his arm around me. "A few thousand years, give or take. Unlike made vamps, we can't be killed by stake or sunlight."

"Or a bullet," I muttered, thinking of my father.

"Doug was staked, Sweetheart. I cleaned up his ashes, then I found a homeless person to replace the missing body and compelled the medical examiner to claim it was a bullet, otherwise there would have been too many questions."

"Oh. I hope we find the blonde bitch so you can take her head."

"The blonde bitch?" Laurent asked.

"The one who turned Dinah."

A phone rang, and Laurent tossed it back to Luke. "That's Darius's phone."

"And if we answer, she'll know he failed."

"Maybe not." I took the phone and hit the green icon. "H-hello?" I answered, making my voice waver.

"Dinah? Where's Darius?" the woman growled, and Luke stiffened next to me.

"He's dead," I whispered. "Some vamps ganged up on him when they saw me kill a human."

"Where are you?" the woman demanded.

"Driving around. I was scared they were going to kill me too, so I stole a car."

"How did you get Darius's phone?"

Shit. "I- I ran off and waited until the vamps left, then I went back for him, but h-he turned to ash. I took his phone to call you, but I couldn't unlock it. I'm sc-scared. And so hungry, but I don't want to kill anyone else. Where are you? Can I come back? I don't want to be alone."

"Did you happen to grab the sword?"

"N-no. I didn't see it."

"Fuck," she hissed. "I'll text you the address. If the phone locks again, the passcode is 6969."

"Got it. Thank you, uh... What's your name?"

"Just get here." With that she disconnected.

"I will end that bitch," Luke seethed as his claws dug into my arm. "I will cut her traitorous head from her body but not before I rip out her lying fucking tongue."

I scooted as far as I could across the back seat, leaning against the door. I didn't think Luke meant to hurt me, but it was like his wrath was my own. It must be the bond we shared. He snapped his red eyes my direction, and I cringed.

"Dinah, Sweetheart?"

"You… Uh, I can feel your anger. In here." I tapped my chest.

He scrubbed a hand down his face. "Fuck. Did I hurt you?" His pleading eyes were once again violet.

"No." That was a lie, but the pain had receded quickly.

"I did. Just like you can feel my pain or anger, I can feel your emotions as well. Please forgive me."

I nodded because I believed him. "I forgive you. Uh, I take it you recognized the voice?"

"Yes. That was my assistant, Arabella."

Darius's phone pinged, and I unlocked it using the passcode she'd given me. Since I didn't know the area, I passed the phone to Luke. After he read it, he squeezed the phone so hard, it shattered. I squeaked, and Laurent pulled over and put the car in park.

"What it is?" Laurent asked, turning in his seat.

"She's at Doug's. I should have assumed that after the guards there were killed. Laurent, I want you to take Dinah back to my house while I dispose of this cunt."

"No!" I grabbed Luke's arm. "I want to be there. She killed my father, and she turned me. Made me into this…" I huffed. "I want to watch her die." A different type of pain coursed through my body – sadness. It wasn't my own considering I was angry, so I looked over at Luke. "What?"

"You're upset that she turned you."

"Of course I fucking am. If anyone was going to turn me it should have been you." I crossed my arms over my chest and gazed out the window.

Luke leaned over and grabbed me, pulling me onto his lap. He buried his face in my neck. "I should have known. Lillith wouldn't give me someone who didn't want to be with me for eternity."

"What's it going to be?" Laurent asked.

Luke sighed, his breath warm against my skin. "Dinah deserves to watch." I felt I deserved to participate, but before I could say so, Luke gave Laurent the address, and after putting it in the navigation system, he pulled back onto the road. I would get to see the house my father had left me, but I doubted I would want to keep it after the night was over. The closer we got, the more I wanted to end the blonde, and I told Luke as much. After arguing back and forth, we finally agreed on how to proceed once we reached my house. Then I fed from his wrist briefly when the thirst got to be too much.

Laurent parked on the next street over. He got out, waiting on Luke to do the same. Luke buried his face against my neck again. "Do not underestimate Arabella. Do not go off script."

"I've got this," I promised. He kissed me hard before joining Laurent on the sidewalk. I moved to the driver's seat of Laurent's car we'd stopped to get since Arabella would recognize Luke's. Using the GPS, I drove the rest of the way, parking on the street. I stared at the house my father had called home. It was a white three-story with sage green shutters, surrounded by an ornate wrought-iron fence. It was gorgeous. Taking a breath, I got out and stopped at the gate. Luke informed me about the code needed to gain entry, but I needed Arabella to think I was out of my head. I pushed on the gate, and when it didn't open, I shook it. "No, no, no." I took a step back, looking around. If she was watching out the window, I needed to be convincing. Huffing, I vaulted the gate and landed with a wobble. The front door opened, and she stared at me.

"I need your help. I almost stopped to…" I looked around again, then whispered, "Get a drink. Can I get something from you? I'm so thirsty."

"Get your ass inside," she hissed.

"Yes. Inside. Coming." I rushed but not too quickly. Arabella held the door open, and I launched myself at her. She stumbled trying to get away from me. "I need to feed. Please," I begged.

Arabella shoved me, and I went down on my ass, which pissed me off, but I pretended to be sad. "Why'd you do that?"

She towered over me with her hands on her hips. "How are you clean? And who's shirt is that?"

"I had to get the blood off. It was itchy, so I dunked my head in someone's pool."

"And the shirt?" she asked with narrowed eyes.

"I-I found it. Please, I'm so hungry."

"I'll feed you," a man said, entering the room. I had been under the misconception that all vampires were stunning. This one wasn't. Or maybe this was the glamour of the hour. Either way, I didn't want him anywhere near me.

"Who are you?" I asked, climbing to my feet.

"Montrose Halligan, at your service." He bent at the waist, bowing like an English gentleman.

"Montrose. Is that a family name? I was named after

79

Dinah Washington, a jazz singer from the fifties. Have you heard of her? My father was a big fan. I say was because she killed him," I said, pointing at Arabella. "Was that your doing, Montrose? Did you have Dinah kill my father? I think she did it because she was a jealous bitch."

Arabella shrieked, "Of course I was fucking jealous. I gave Lukas everything, but to him, I was nothing but someone to boss around. The club should have been mine. This house should have been mine. But instead, he gave everything to a washed-up musician."

I looked around as though I didn't know it was my father's house. "Well, it's my house now, so I want you out of here."

Arabella laughed, and that pissed me off. She thought because she'd turned me that she was stronger. She wasn't. I had Luke's blood in me. Using my newfound speed, I rushed her, grabbed her by the throat, and lifted her off her feet, slamming her onto her back.

"Let her go," Montrose commanded.

I slowly turned my head, my gaze turning red. "No."

His eyebrows shot up, and I dropped my fangs. He then took a step toward me, but a sexy voice stopped him.

"I wouldn't do that if I were you." Luke, having masked his presence, swung at the other Ancient's neck when he turned around. The decapitated head should have made me queasy. It didn't. I focused on the blonde bitch trying to get out of my grasp.

Luke stood next to me, staring down at his assistant. "Move back, Sweetheart." I did as he asked, and Arabella jumped to her feet.

"Lukas, please," she begged.

Luke swung the sword, slicing from her neck to her groin. "That was for being a duplicitous bitch." He then closed the distance and kicked her so hard she hit the wall ten feet away. Luke followed, driving the sword into her chest, pinning her to the wall. When she tried to claw him, he broke both her wrists. I cringed at the crunch of bones, but it was also satisfying. Luke grabbed her jaws and wrench them open, pulling her tongue out. Using a claw, he sliced it off and tossed it on the floor. I was glad Luke had a cleaning service because that was nasty. "That was for turning on me after all these years." He used his bloody nail to slice open her face. "That's for the hell of it. But this?" He removed the sword from her chest, blood dripping everywhere. "This is for killing my best friend." With one swing, Arabella's head was separated from her shoulders, and it fell to the side with a thud onto the hardwood floor.

I stalked over, grabbed the sword from Luke, and shoved it into her torso. "And that's for turning me without asking!" I stabbed her several times before Laurent coughed. I hadn't heard him come in.

"I think you got her."

"Damn right I did." Turning to Luke, I asked, "This is my house now?"

He was a sight with blood splatter covering his hands. Some had gotten on his face, so I walked over and rubbed it off with my thumb.

"Yeah, Sweetheart, this is your house."

"I don't think I want it after this."

"I don't blame you. I'll have it cleaned up, and you can put it on the market."

"I'll buy it," Laurent offered. When I frowned at him, he grinned. "What? It's a great house."

CHAPTER SEVEN

Lukas – Four Months Later

"DINAH?" I CALLED up the stairs. We were supposed to be meeting Laurent at The Limelight to check out the new saxophone player he had hired. After a long discussion, she and I decided to sell the club. It didn't hold any appeal to her, and for me? The memories of all the nights Doug and I shared there were still raw. Like with Doug's house, my brother asked if he could take the club off our hands. When I asked about his territory, he said his second had it under control. I think he was just lonely and wanted to be around family.

"Sweetheart?" I called again. When she didn't answer, I strode up the stairs to find my beloved. Dinah had done remarkably well with her blood thirst. We had been able to travel to Nashville and pack up her apartment two weeks after she'd been turned. I paid to get her out of the lease early, and other than her clothes, she donated the rest of her things to a local homeless charity. In those same two weeks, she and I spent most of our time in bed, making love, feeding from the other, and just being. It was an amazing fourteen days. In all my time on earth, I had never felt as alive as I did when I was balls deep in my beloved. Each time we came together was different as our bond became stronger. Each time, I learned something new about the woman I couldn't get enough of. Like anytime I wore a suit, it was coming off quickly if Dinah had a say in the matter. She called it suit porn. It was a good thing I was a wealthy and could afford to replace the ones she shredded with her claws.

When I reached our bedroom, Dinah was sitting on the side of the bed in her lacy underwear, staring at nothing. I crossed the room and knelt in front of her, taking her hands in mine. "Sweetheart?"

"It just hit me. I'll never have children," she whispered. In the four months we'd been together, she'd never mentioned wanting kids.

"You can't give birth, no, but if you want a child, I'll get you one."

She morphed from sad to mortified. "You'd steal a baby for me?"

I chuckled and tucked a long, dark lock of hair behind her ear. "No, but I would adopt one for you."

"Really?" Her eyes filled with pink-tinged tears.

"I would give you anything your heart desired, My Beloved. You should know that." Using my thumbs, I wiped away the wetness.

"I do know, and I am so thankful to be yours."

"Should we start the process?"

Dinah bit her lip and shook her head. "Not yet. Now that I know it's an option, I'm no longer sad." She stood, pushing me back against the dresser, gripping the lapels of my jacket. "Do you know what I am, Mr. Benoit?" Her fangs extended, and she scraped them along the edge of my jaw.

I grasped her plump ass with both hands and angled my head, giving her access to my neck. "Tell me, Mrs. Benoit."

"I'm starving," she hissed before she struck. Did I mention how erotic it was when Dinah drank from me? Needless to say, my suit was ruined, and we were late meeting Laurent.

When we did arrive, me in a fresh suit and Dinah in a form-fitting red dress that accentuated her ample curves, Laurent rolled his eyes. He was used to us never arriving on time, but as much as he complained about it, there was a longing behind his teasing. I often found him staring at Dinah. Not in a way that raised my hackles, but such that I knew he wanted what I had. When you lived for an eternity, bedding strangers lost its appeal after a while. He greeted Dinah with a kiss to her cheek, then he took my hand, pulling me into a tight embrace. My coven was still unaware that we were Ancients, and I saw no need to change that. Speaking of my coven, I had thrown a gala to announce my queen. She was received with equal amounts of awe and respect. Even the female vamps had swarmed her with kindness instead of bitterness. Many had vied for my attention over the years, but once they met my beloved and were hit with her essence, they could feel my power flowing through her veins. No, she wasn't an Ancient, but she came as close as possible without having been created.

The Limelight hadn't reopened as planned after I originally met with Dinah. Arabella failed to contact the employees. When Laurent mentioned taking over, Dinah handed him the reins and told him to do with the club as he wished. He took a few weeks to remodel the interior while continuing to pay the employees, meeting with each one to get to know them. I joined him for the first meeting, officially retiring as manager, and reassuring my former coworkers they would enjoy working for my brother. If possible, the club was even more popular under Laurent's guidance.

He led us to our reserved four-top, and we enjoyed a night of drinks and excellent music. The new saxophonist was on par with Doug, and the crowd sat enthralled as he played. I looked around at familiar faces as well as new ones, proud of what Doug and I had started all those years ago. My beloved had never been a fan of jazz, and that was due to her father's abandonment. She felt he chose his music over his family, and even though she knew better now, it had tainted her view. She was softening to my favorite genre after realizing why Doug had disappeared. I shared stories of her father so she could know the man he had been. I often found her talking to the urn that held a place of honor in our home.

Before meeting Dinah, if someone had asked me would I miss tending bar every night, the answer would have been an unequivocal yes. But now? Now my nights were filled with music of a different kind. Dinah and I danced in the kitchen to whatever song she queued up on her phone while she cooked our favorite foods. She was still getting used to eating again, but small quantities were manageable. We drove around our city with the radio playing softly from the car's surround sound while checking on our coven members. We stopped off at the casino where my woman played blackjack for hours while I cheered her on. We snuggled on the sofa in front of a fire, sipping wine, while the stereo provided background noise.

My life was bursting at the seams, and as happy as I was with Dinah in my life? I was even deadlier than before.

THE END

Author's Note

I was writing a different book when the characters decided to become difficult, so I set it aside and began perusing various stories I had dabbled in. I opened *The Limelight,* what was previously going to be a contemporary series featuring four sisters. The premise was the same – their father passed away, leaving the club to them. Wanting to write something short and in time for Halloween, Lukas and Dinah's novella was born. Getting a story across in 20k words isn't easy, but I am happy with how this one turned out, and I hope you enjoyed it. If you've read my other books, you've seen New Orleans pop up every now and then. I love this city. I wrote another paranormal short story, *Voodoo Lovin',* set in NOLA for an anthology way back in 2014 that you can read for free on my website, www.faithgibsonauthor.com/freereads

ABOUT THE AUTHOR

Multi-genre author Faith Gibson began writing in high school, and through the years, penned many stories and poems. Since she was a child, her dreams (and sometimes nightmares) were vivid constructs, making her shake her head and ask, "where the hell did that come from?" Many of these nighttime escapades have led to a line, a chapter, or even a complete story.

"Love is love, and there's not enough love in the world." This belief she holds strongly, and it's the prevailing theme in her works, all of which come with a happy ending.

Faith believes her purpose in life is to entertain the masses, even if it's one person at a time. Aspirations of becoming a rock 'n' roll drummer didn't come to fruition, but she's fulfilling a different dream, and that's bringing stories to life one book at a time.

Faith lives just outside of Nashville, Tennessee, with the love of her life and her American Staffordshire pup, Luna, the writing partner. When she's not hard at work writing her next adventure, Faith can often be found reading, cooking up something in the kitchen, listening to live music, or off on an adventure of her own.

www.ingramcontent.com/pod-product-compliance
Lightning Source LLC
Chambersburg PA
CBHW070522130626
46555CB00003B/1308